About the Author

Jamie Smartkins, lead software professional and a voracious reader and avid lover of music of all genres since childhood. Winner of several quiz and dance competitions since college days. Jamie started writing about fantasy, fiction stories as he believes creative art in any genre is the ultimate form of abstract science. He has passion to learn new languages and can speak seven languages. He is tremendously inspired by the work of Suzanne Collins, Stephenie Meyer and Charles Dickens in the world of writing.

https://jamiesmartkins.com

Jexter Bladebrace and
The Exalted Kingdom

Jamie Smartkins

Jexter Bladebrace and The Exalted Kingdom

Olympia Publishers
London

www.olympiapublishers.com
OLYMPIA PAPERBACK EDITION

A CIP catalogue record for this title is
available from the British Library.

ISBN: 978-1-78830-404-7

This is a work of fiction.
Names, characters, places and incidents originate from the writer's
imagination. Any resemblance to actual persons, living or dead, is
purely coincidental.

First Published in 2022

Olympia Publishers
Tallis House
2 Tallis Street
London
EC4Y 0AB
Printed in Great Britain

Dedication

I dedicate this book to all the teenagers and young adult readers around the globe who at some point in their daily life feels mundane, should experience fun, thrill and excitement in every phase of life and that should be the motivation of every individual to achieve greater heights in both personal and professional level.

Acknowledgements

My sincere thanks to the entire editorial team and the entire publishing, designing, marketing team for making this book reach out to mass audience.

Ominoulada Attack on Earth

It was the year 2080 AD. An asteroid named Ominoulada was making its move since 2075 from a galaxy, Galactotitan, situated 20000 light years away from solar system. Scientists, analysts around the globe, predicted this catastrophic attack on planet Earth and by all means got prepared to destroy the asteroid as soon as it comes in contact with stratosphere. Every military, cavalry around the globe got ready to be a savior of human civilization as the asteroid was so far the biggest foreign object ever to hit Earth. The asteroid was supposed to be as big as one-fourth the size of Earth. Impact of that size would completely annihilate the planet Earth. Every life on the planet was threatened. NASA confirmed the asteroid had arrived in the solar system traversing Pluto at lightning speed. The military, airships, fighter jets around the globe from Russia, UK, Japan, China, US, India, Korea, Australia triggered the missiles all together, capable of demolishing the asteroid before it reaches the Earth's surface. The history of mankind was witnessing the biggest assault of heavenly object. 25 May, 2080, early morning people were glued to television and several went up to terrace, roofs of the buildings to witness the missiles propelling up to the space. People were petrified and everyone started praying to God. Gigantic black shadows of clouds engulfed the sky across earth as the asteroid was approaching close to stratosphere, trying to devour the planet Earth. As soon as Ominoulada came close to stratosphere, the missiles from all around the globe flew up and made a thunderous impact on the asteroid and nearly managed to break the asteroid into pieces. The broken pieces were turned into debris and disappeared in atmosphere but a cruel fate decided something else. One big chunk got broken from Ominoulada and now racing towards Earth with full speed. Nothing could be done this time as all the missiles had been used up. People were watching helplessly the monstrous piece of burning rock freely falling on Earth. The broken piece of asteroid hit the Earth badly and the entire planet shivered. It was dead silence everywhere. The continental plates shifted apart, several continents were submerged under oceans. Is it the end of civilization?

Jexter in Search of Life

Fifteen days after Ominoulada hit the earth, Jexter opened his eyes and looked at the sky. He could only see dense fumes engulfing the sky, sea birds, and vultures, flying around. He thought he was dreaming, he turned sideways and just felt an excruciating pain in his left arm. The sight of bleeding left him flabbergasted and numb. His left arm was bleeding profusely and one of his fingers in his left hand was chopped off. He cried in pain and looked aside, he could only see corpses and remembered the Ominoulada attack. He didn't know where exactly he was situated, his smart phone was missing. He could only see abandoned ships, submarines in broken condition around him lying on land. He was sitting on an island surrounded by a vast ocean. Jexter still couldn't believe what he was going through. With his arm broken, he started shouting, "Anybody here? Anybody still alive?" and made terrible sounds to catch attention. Even if animals alive should respond to him. His intuitive mind told him he was not the only one to be alive in this apocalyptic world. He started running in search of company. He couldn't find anybody. His mind was choking, but he wouldn't give up. He was hungry as hell. He saw most of the trees were burned down. One of the trees nearby was having fruits, all half burnt. He just climbed up the tree and ate as much burnt fruits as possible to quench his appetite. He vomited but still ate. He then tried to have a look from the top of the tree. He couldn't believe his eyes. He could see the water was soon filling up the island. The island was going to be submerged underwater soon. He quickly jumped from the tree and went to the marooned ship near him and saw a small life boat. He went inside the ship and saw many barrels of food, fruits, cheese, beer cans. A sigh of temporary relief. At least he could eat enough before surrendering to the natural calamity. He took most of them, as much as possible to fill up the boat. With humongous effort he managed to push the boat in the sea. He started rowing the boat hard to get into deep waters. He looked back and saw the entire island was engulfed by the ocean. He managed to stay alive but didn't know how long he would survive in the sea. He kept rowing the boat and went into deep waters.

Jexter Encounters Spectrovor

Jexter kept rowing for nearly 10 days at sea, in search of a landmass, surviving on the food he carried in the boat. His food was nearly finished. Jexter fought the storms, heavy winds, and high tidal waves of the sea by sheer courage and grit. He knew he wouldn't survive long enough and he desperately needed to find a landmass. His body started giving up, he looked pale and had no energy to sail the boat under the scorching heat of the sun. He was about to give up his hope of survival but suddenly he noticed a weird phenomenon happening from the back of his boat. The water behind the boat was creating ripples like big concentric waves in large areas, as if something was trying to come out from under water. He steered his boat back to see what was happening in the water around him. He couldn't steer the boat close to it as the current from the epicenter of the ripple was pushing Jexter's boat away. Jexter thought it might be an earthquake happening underwater but he was dare enough to drive near to it. Soon a large super-advanced vehicle popped out above the water. Jexter fell from the boat due to strong force of turbines of the vehicle. Jexter tried to swim afloat and saw the vehicle lifted above water and he tried to decode what was that thing that just came out of underwater. It looked like a spaceship for sure, as Jexter had seen spaceship in movies. The name of the spaceship read as Spectrovor. Jexter desperately wanted to get into the vehicle Spectrovor. His boat already capsized and this spaceship was his last hope. He didn't know what was there inside the spaceship, whether any humans or aliens? He didn't care; whoever was there inside that spaceship, he would seek help. Thus he shouted loudly for help while swimming to stay afloat. But the sound of turbine was so loud, Jexter's voice was doomed to oblivion. As the Spectrovor kept circulating around the ripples on water to gather momentum to fly above, Jexter fortunately managed to pounce on one of the wings of the spaceship and clung on to it. The spaceship took off and started flying above the sea. Jexter nearly got asphyxiated by the crazy winds that blew on him as he held the wing of the spaceship tightly. He looked down and he could only see ocean. When Spectrovor reached higher altitude he could see lot of landmasses destroyed and submerged under the sea. After long travel over the ocean, the Spectrovor started making a descent on a landmass. Jexter understood the spaceship was making a landing and he quickly jumped off the spaceship and fell on the water near the shore. Spectrovor landed on the island. Jexter kept swimming near the shore to reach the land. Jexter could hear lot of loud noises. Was it sound of humans or animals? He was excited and happy to feel he was not the sole survivor. But he was scared about the spaceship, which he thought would contain aliens who might be a threat to the surviving humans or animals in that unknown island of Earth.

Spectropeans Give Earthlings an Offer

Hearing the sound of spaceship landing, the people from the forest came outside to witness what was happening around. Nearly a hundred people came out of the forest, looking petrified. Jexter hiding behind the wooden logs staying afloat in shallow waters near the shore and watching silently. Jexter saw most of the people were from different tribes and ethnicity. A tall well-built man came forward and had a look at the spaceship. He looked fearless, ready to confront the spaceship. The people followed him. He seemed to be the leader of the group. He started shouting at the spaceship in colloquial, abusive language unknown to Jexter. The Spectrovor spaceship gate opened. A group of 10 people came out of the spaceship with heavily-armed high-octane weapons in their hands. Everyone watching them in horror. Jexter was now convinced those people were aliens covered in silver metallic masks and metallic suits. While the aliens marched in front, sound from spaceship Spectrovor echoed around. "No need to fear, Earthlings, we are here to protect you."

The tall guy came and shouted. "Who are you?"

The answer came from Spectrovor in a very strong resonating voice. "We are Spectropeans, natives of Spectronom Galaxy situated 10000 light years from your galaxy. We have just send our people to help you out. Kindly follow what they ask you to do."

The tall man, whose name was Mac, gazed at the ten masked aliens with suspicious eyes. He then stared at the spaceship and said, "Why would you help us and why would we trust you?"

The answer came from Spectrovor. "We had a premonition from our galaxy that Earth is going to be destroyed by Ominoulada impact. We had orders to rescue you Earthlings, natives of planet Earth."

Mac yelled, "Under whose orders you came to Earth? We are capable of saving our people. We don't need aliens to interfere, just go back from where you came from."

Spectrovor responded by saying, "We are not allowed to say under whose orders we came. One thing we can say: this is the only landmass left to be submerged underwater. Every other landmasses of your planet Earth is under the ocean. This landmass will also be under the ocean in three weeks' time. The choice is yours."

Mac again yelled and told Spectrovor to go back to their galaxy. The ten masked aliens, without saying a word, went back to the Spectrovor and within seconds the gates of the spaceship closed and Spectrovor flew off and disappeared within the sky.

Jexter's Proposal of Solution of Survival on Island

Jexter in the meantime watched everything. As soon the Spectrovor left, he came running to Mac, saying, "Hello, Monsieur! Thank God I found some people alive out here and I was in boat for days to reach here."

Mac was irritated by his behavior and angrily said, "Mate, are you one of them from spaceship which just landed or some moron thanking God that we are still alive? If you are one of us humans, we got to stick together as a team and find a way to protect this island from going under water. So you better stop talking nonsense and start moving."

Jexter grinned and said politely, "I am Jexter! Jexter Bladebrace." Jexter was then introduced to the survivors by Mac. Jexter understood that Mac was the leader of the survivors on the island. There were nearly 100 survivors. Mac told Jexter that ninety percent of the people do not understand English but everybody understood each other well by body language and gestures. Mac told Jexter these 100 people were a family. They were going to stick together till last breath to protect this island. Mac called everyone for meeting to decide what could be the next step of action. He did not want aliens to help them in such precarious situation. Besides, how could they trust aliens? Mac asked everybody to come up with ideas how to stop the flood from submerging the island. People started thinking for some time, but none came up with a proper solution. Mac got angry and rebuked everyone. Everyone was upset with Mac's attitude. Jexter tried to pacify the situation by proposing an idea that together they could build a dam which could stop the water from entering the island. Mac smiled back and people cheered for Jexter, thinking that they got a solution. Jexter felt like a hero. Soon from the crowd, a female voice interrupted. "That's probably the worst idea I have ever heard."

Mac got enraged and wanted answer from the concerned person. A beautiful lady in her twenties came in front and yelled, "I said."

Mac asked sarcastically, "Who are you? How can you challenge the idea of building dam? Are you a scientist?"

The lady responded "I am Shelly. I am not a scientist but an archaeologist. The idea of building a dam won't save this island. Suppose even if we build a dam and prevent water from entering island, there can be a possibility of earthquake, who knows?" Shelly continued. "Besides, building dam is not a small task. It will nearly take a month to build using all the manpower. Now you tell me in what way the idea of building seems feasible?"

Mac was baffled and looked at Jexter. Jexter reluctantly admitted Shelly's point, maybe she was right. Mac then asked Shelly if she had any solution to the situation.

Shelly promptly said, "Let's join hands with aliens, they seem to help us. We have nothing left. You rejected their offer, now repent to avoid complete annihilation of human species."

Mac was in no mood to join hands with Spectrovor. He clearly said that and ordered everyone to start building the dam. Jexter also felt Shelly was right, so he tried to persuade Mac, but Mac gave deaf ear to him. Everyone started working together to build the dam. They cut down trees, took the wood and started working day and night. All the men put every bit of their energy into building the dam. Mac and Jexter were leading from the front. The women bought fruits for the men working. Shelly brought some fruits for Jexter. Jexter's finger was still bleeding. Shelly noticed and felt bad for Jexter and helped Jexter dress his wound. Jexter thanked Shelly. Jexter felt Shelly was a generous beautiful lady. Shelly smiled and left. The dam was finished after two weeks of stupendous effort. Everyone was excited and happy. Mac called everybody and said he was very satisfied with everyone's effort in making the island a perfect place for living. Everyone clapped and cheered for Mac and Jexter. Within moments, everyone felt a tremor in the island. Holes started appearing in the dam. Everyone looked at each other in disbelief that in spite of putting mammoth effort into building the dam, nature had gone against them. They were now sure if the tremor continued to happen for some more time, the island would soon sink under the sea: the dam would be of no use. One of the people, frustrated, came in the middle and looked up into the sky with sad eyes and chanted,

Yosh yosh shomane lego bouy!
Yosh yosh tozeba meno souy.

Nobody understood what he said but one thing they understood for sure he was cursing nature. Soon all the people started chanting the same thinking it may change their fate.

Yosh yosh shomane lego bouy!
Yosh yosh tozeba meno souy.

The island was still having the tremors. They could see some holes appearing in the dam. Everyone was just waiting to be swallowed by sea. They realized they won't be able to cheat death this time. They looked into the sky and prayed. They saw Spectrovor was hovering around the island and landed. Here came the voice from Spectrovor, "We told you, you have no other choice Earthlings. We can protect you from this situation."

Mac replied submissively, "Yes, lord! save me and my people. We will be your slaves forever." The Spectrovor clarified Mac by saying the Earthlings should treat Spectropeans as their allies, not their master.

Shelly asked Spectrovor inquisitively, "How can you save us? Do you want to take us to your galaxy? We may not survive there also."

The Spectrovor responded by saying "We have a temporary solution, soon you will get to know." One of the Spectropeans from Spectrovor got down and marched towards the people with a glowing wand in hand. He then looked at Jexter and asked him to come towards him. Jexter went close to the alien. The Spectropean lifted his glowing wand and pressed a button and a sharp needle came from the top of the glowing wand. Immediately fluorescent light of the stick dispersed, making everyone nearly blind. The Spectropean injected the needle of the wand into Jexter's neck. Jexter immediately collapsed to the ground, whining in pain. Now what the people saw was unbelievable.

Earthlings Undergoes Transformation

Something was happening in Jexter's body. It looked like Jexter was transforming into something. People were transfixed with horror, watching Jexter's transformation. Jexter's heart was beating heavily as if it was going to blast anytime. Jexter's eyes were becoming bigger in size and ears were disappearing. The legs were transforming into joint appendages. Jexter yelled furiously, "What have you done to me? Have you turned me into a beast?"

"You are now a humphibian. You can now live on both land as well as in water. In land you will be human and under water you will be a fishman, just like the fish," the Spectropean explained.

"Oh my Gosh, why would you do that?" Jexter shouted back to Spectropean.

The Spectropean tried to calm down Jexter and said, "This is the only solution to prevent human extinction from the planet. We have tried this test on you. Now you have to jump in water and see your potential of survival under water."

Jexter couldn't believe what he just heard from Spectropean. But he felt like jumping into water. He dragged himself towards the shore and jumped into water. Soon he disappeared.

People thought Jexter might have drowned. Everyone was anxiously waiting for Jexter's return. Shelly was very upset and tried to hit the alien, thinking that he killed her friend by making him a mutant. The alien pushed her aside softly without harming her and assured them Jexter would be back and the longer Jexter stayed underwater, the better would be the chance of success in protecting the human race.

As the sun was setting down, everyone now felt that Jexter had been drowned. Suddenly one kid from the crowd pointed to the air near the shore and said, "Look there." They could see Jexter swimming and jumping above the sea like a dolphin.

Jexter then came to the shore with his webbed feet and couldn't stand properly. He was breathing hard and the Spectropean went close to him and said, "Now try thinking you are human, you will be human again." Jexter started to focus himself as human being and soon he could see he was again transforming to normal human being. Everyone went crazy after watching Jexter transforming back to his normal self.

They asked the alien, "Are you from heaven? Are you an Angel or something?"

The Spectropean clarified, "No, we are just like you Earthlings, a bit different than you all as in our dimension we use power of brain and mind to maximise the potential of discovering things which may be unthinkable on your planet. In our planet, everything is quite possible. Now who's ready to become next humphibian after Jexter?"

Shelly came forward. Jexter was happy to see Shelly.

"Hope you gonna make me into beautiful mermaid," Shelly quipped.

The alien curiously asked, "Exactly. How you know it?"

Shelly smiled and said sarcastically, "On our planet, women can use their power of mind to predict things accurately."

Alien appreciated and repeated the same process as given to Jexter. Shelly transformed into a beautiful mermaid. Jexter wished Shelly good luck for her journey in the sea. Shelly sneaked into the sea and disappeared. Shelly returned after quite some time and she remembered that after arrival in the shore one had to think of own self as human, then the person would be transformed back to human. She tried to focus and successfully transformed into old self. Jexter was delighted to see Shelly back. He went to Shelly and hugged her in excitement. Shelly assured Jexter she was doing fine. The alien wasted no time in injecting all the Earthlings, including Mac, and transformed them into humphibians. All the Earthlings made a test drive of their own performances under the sea by transforming themselves into fishmen and mermaids the moment they dived underwater. Everyone returned to island and transformed back to human mode. The aliens warned everyone to be prepared for imminent tidal wave and possible earthquake, so that they could transform immediately to fishman and mermaids.

"If we are going to be underwater, how long can we stay underwater? We need to have shelter under water. Do we have a house underneath?" Mac retorted. "What if the sharks or ferocious sea animals attack us? What are we going to do?"

"You will have to think like a dolphin underwater. Use your brain for survival. Regarding shelter, we will help you to build one underwater," the Spectropean said.

Mac curiously asked, "When are we going to meet again?"

"Pretty soon," answered the Spectropean.

Last Week on the Landmass for Earthlings

The Spectrovor soon left. Before leaving, the alien handed a supersonic gun to Jexter and told him to use underwater in case of sudden attack by predators. All humans were now humphibians. They could now remain as humans on landmass and transform into fishmen and mermaids underwater. In the meantime everyone started practising what it was like to stay underwater, went together just like a shoal of fish. Jexter and Shelly went together underwater in search of shelter. Jexter and Shelly transformed into fishman and mermaid and began their journey underwater. They were moving at great speeds underwater. They went in deep waters, chased by sharks many times but managed to deceive them. They were trying to find shelters underground. They found one big ship deep down below at the bottom of the ocean. They went inside to have a look. The ship might have been down below the ocean for over 100 years.

It had a huge space and they thought it to be a perfect place for the humphibians to settle there. They looked at each other and agreed this could be the place for underwater stay. They swam up and reached the island. Shelly and Jexter called Mac and had some intense discussions regarding their journey under ocean. Mac listened to them carefully and finally asked them how long could they stay underwater. Jexter responded that the Spectrovor might have an answer to it. Everyone in island was getting mentally prepared to survive underwater. That night, when everyone asleep, Shelly and Jexter staring at the sky on the beach, pondering about the unknown challenges awaiting them. Shelly liked Jexter very much. Jexter could see her feelings for him through her eyes. But she could not confess her love for Jexter as the entire human race was in danger. This would not be right time as they should focus on the upcoming challenges. Jexter could read Shelly's thoughts. But Jexter too didn't reveal his feelings for Shelly. Jexter comforted Shelly that everything would be normal and to have faith in God.

Only time would tell what was in store for Earthlings in near future.

Survival Under the Ocean

The next day was a sunny morning. Everyone woke up with great hope. Mac alerted everyone to be careful underwater as there would be dangerous predators and everyone should stay close to Jexter. Jexter possessed the supersonic gun given to him by the alien. All the hundred people nodded and decided to stick around Jexter till they got their shelter. Jexter and Shelly told them they had found a shelter deep down the ocean, like a sunken ship which could be a temporary place of residence. Everyone was worried. No one knew what future was awaiting the Earthlings underwater. They were praying only to stay much longer on island. One fine day after two weeks, a tremor was felt by Earthlings and before realizing the magnitude, the island went down under water. The people immediately transformed into water species viz fishmen and mermaids and swam in a flock under the ocean following Jexter, Shelly and Mac. In the meantime, they were attacked by dangerous sea animals, but Jexter's supersonic gun protected all the fishmen and mermaids. They reached the bottom of the ocean where the shipwreck was situated. Jexter and Shelly led them to one of the chambers inside the ship. All of them agreed to stay there. One big problem they were having was communication, as they were doing gestures to communicate with each other. One thing for sure: they wanted to talk but couldn't. Suddenly Jexter looked into Shelly's eyes and could understand what was going through Shelly's mind. In other words, he could contact Shelly telepathically and understand. Even Shelly could hear Jexter's inner voice. First they tried to block the windows and doors. This was miraculously done by the supersonic gun which was used to ward off the predators. Now the magical supersonic gun could also produce tar or could camouflage anything. They blocked the entrance and the windows of the chambers where all them could relax without fear. It seemed they wanted to eat something. Now they were no more humans on water, they went out of the sunken ship and searched for plankton, small fish and fed on them. Time passed so slowly.

Thespon Discussing with Spectropeans Regarding Earth

Spaceship Spectrovor reached the Spectronom galaxy and landed on their planet. The aliens were closely monitoring the Earthlings, the fishmen and mermaids on earth from their magical mirror in the spacecraft. They were discussing how long the Earthlings were going to stay under water.

Thespon, the captain of Spectrovor from Spectronom Galaxy, as well as leader of the alien planet said to his fellow Spectropeans, "Guys, just wait and watch. Earth is still undergoing major changes. Our scientific labs are suggesting earth is in metamorphosed state. Let's see what major changes come. If something worse happens, we are going to retrieve the Earthlings in our galaxy. The human species shall not become extinct."

The Earthlings were leading the life of water species, they were communicating via telepathy and gestures. They were tremendously dissatisfied with their aquatic life. They couldn't even cry under water. Their hearts were still the same, having the same emotions but unable to cry. Only change was the addition of gills as well as lungs, to breathe under water. They kept swimming under the ocean.

Once it happened that Shelly kept swimming under water and soon went too far from the sunken ship. Shelly, unnerved, kept searching for landmass, or town or city where the human species could dwell but couldn't find one. While moving fast under the oceans she hit a rock and fell below and kept falling and hit the lowest point on the sea bed and lost consciousness. Jexter was anxiously waiting for Shelly. It had been quite some time. Immediately Thespon from Spectrovor notified Jexter via supersonic gun where Jexter could see the longitude and latitude with red light blinking. Jexter understood that Spectropean trying to convene something to him. He immediately rushed towards the location. He swam and swam, killed two deadly sharks in the midway and finally arrived at the location. He found Shelly in unconscious state on the ocean bed. He got scared as Shelly was not moving. He shook Shelly severely and slapped her. Miraculously Shelly was back to her senses. She had a mild concussion with the hit on the rocks. Jexter was delighted and he hugged Shelly tightly and kissed her forehead. Shelly was delighted to see Jexter. They were travelling back to their ship of residence.

Thespon from Spectrovor got elated, looking into the magical mirror and said, "These guys are made for each other. These two guys have unfinished mission left to be achieved." The aliens asked Thespon what was the mission the two earthlings, Jexter and Shelly, had to achieve. Thespon responded them to have patience to get the answer as he was not going to reveal the answer to them.

Soon the Earthlings got settled in the sunken ship. They now began to feel like actual fish, although their hearts were still beating like humans'. What a life they were having underwater. There have no work, no payment, no innovation. Only job they have now was finding food and survival from predators and finally getting back to the shelter: the ship. How long could they continue like this? They needed to be in a proper place of habitat, should transform into human beings and live like humans, be among a human civilization in this apocalyptic world.

Journey to Spectronom

One thing surprising to the earthlings was that they felt like they were getting younger underwater. Their eyes glowed brightly under deep water when they searched for food.

They were wondering why the aliens gifted them with these powers. But they needed a landmass. They kept searching for landmass. They swam and jumped above the ocean to see the sky and sun. They couldn't find a single landmass. They kept moving under the ocean beds. Life was going as usual when one fine day Jexter, Shelly and Mac were travelling and exploring underwater and entered such a region near the ocean basin where they couldn't see anything: even their glowing eyes couldn't watch anything. A dense fog was obscuring the place. Should they go inside that zone? Fear struck their heart. But Jexter bravely moved ahead and entered into the thick cloud. Mac and Shelly followed and entered inside and tried to find Jexter. It seemed that Jexter disappeared within blink of an eye. Mac and Shelly looked at each other, wondering where Jexter could vanish within seconds. They moved ahead and suddenly felt in different dimension of world where they were navigating through vacuum at supersonic speed. Before they understood, they saw themselves fall in a barren desert. Shelly looked aside and saw Jexter lying there. They were transformed into humans. Jexter looked baffled and said, "Thank God. You guys are also here, I thought I had lost you guys." Jexter spoke with great pain as his face had now just transformed into human face. He was so happy to speak to his heart's content. So were Shelly and Mac happy to speak. They were trying to think how they reached this desolate island from midst of the deep ocean and soon remembered the dense fog in the midst of ocean from which they arrived in this barren desert. That fog under the ocean bed was the gateway to this desert. But what was this place, where exactly was this situated? They thought this desert might be from Earth and finally they felt ecstatic that they finally found a habitat. Soon they started to explore the desert. They could only see sand dunes, not even trees. The desert was stretched over vast area. They looked at the sky and saw the sky was crystal clear, not even clouds existed. How could the sky be so pure? A star was shining bright in the sky which looked just like the sun but there was difference in the color of light emitted. They walked and walked but couldn't find anybody. After walking straight for a long time, they realized the desert was coming to dead end. They stopped at the dead end and saw the desert was finishing there. They were horrified as they looked down below. They couldn't see anything below.

Seemed like hell down below. They could see a second landmass was situated quite far from the first landmass. But it was impossible to reach the second landmass as there was no bridge in between the two landmasses. If they tried to jump, they would fall below to hell.

They kept pondering around how to reach the second landmass situated the other end. They felt like they were trapped. Suddenly an air vehicle came from nowhere and a voice came from the air vehicle. "Get into the vehicle now." Mac, Jexter and Shelly without uttering any word went inside the air vehicle. They were confined into a separate room. The place looked highly advanced. No doubt Earth technologically advanced before the Ominoulada attack, but this vehicle seemed to be super-advanced as they were being served nice foods, nice suits and nice drinks automatically. Foods from refrigerators coming out and getting poured into dishes. From the wardrobes, nice clothes came flying to them. This made them wonder, are they really on Earth? These things are moving automatically as if they are being driven by someone who is not near to them. Anyways they were amazed but relaxed there. The air vehicle finally landed. They were anxiously waiting for somebody to unlock the door.

Jexter Meets Thespon

After a long wait, the door opened and they saw the masked aliens enter. They were the same masked aliens whom they earlier met on Earth. Lastly, a tall masked alien entered and addressed the Earthlings.

"Welcome to our galaxy, Spectronom. I am Thespon, leader of this planet. This is our planet, Htrae."

Jexter asked Thespon politely, "How we came here? How you pronounce your planet name?"

Thespon replied, "Calm down, Jexter! 'H' is silent when you pronounce our planet. So you can call Trae."

Jexter grinned and said, "What kind of name is that?"

"All your questions will be answered very soon," said Thespon.

Thespon asked Jexter, Shelly and Mac to come along with them outside the air vehicle. They came out together and Jexter was in awe to look outside.

Jexter shouted, "How is this possible? This is my town, my city but this city looks ethereal, so pure, so serene. I can even identify the buildings. Am I still alive? Am I in my dreams? Is this Earth?"

Shelly and Mac were also wondering what Jexter said just now.

Thespon responded, "Your confusions are justifiable. Indeed this looks like your city in Earth. But this is not Earth."

Jexter asked Thespon to remove his mask and show his face and also requested the other aliens to reveal their faces. Thespon silently turned away and removed his mask. Jexter, Mac and Shelly came in front and looked at Thespon. Shelly and Jexter were bewildered to see Thespon. Shelly and Mac then looked at Jexter.

Shelly after a pause questioned Thespon, "You and Jexter are lookalikes. How is that possible? You are from different planet Trae whereas Jexter is from planet Earth."

Thespon smiled back. "Shelly, this is our planet Htrae, which is a clone of your planet Earth. That's the reason behind the name of our planet is Htrae, reverse of your planet Earth and our planet is a mirror image of your planet Earth, if you see through the intergalactic divisional mirror between several galaxies, including your solar system and our Spectronom Galaxy.

Jexter, Shelly and Mac were in awe. They couldn't believe what they just witnessed.

Thespon added, "We can show your Earth from our lab. I know it must be surprising for all three of you. I am Jexter's clone on my planet. Similarly, Shelly, your lookalike is Jezebel, my wife. I will introduce her to you guys later."

Shelly and Jexter looked at each other, baffled and amused.

Jexter had so many questions. He inquisitively asked Thespon, "That means you and I are exactly same person. If I die, then what will happen to you?"

Thespon giggled and said, "Definitely this planet consists of clones of people from planet Earth. But as Earth has now a hundred humphibians left, all other clone species of Earth here died. But being the supreme leader, I possess some ethereal and supernatural powers which the Earthlings may not be familiar with. By the use of these powers, I have revived some of the people of my planet, though not everyone. So it is the quintessential requirement for me to protect you in order to protect myself. Thus I can protect my people in my planet Trae."

"What about our people under sea? Are they okay?" Jexter inquired.

"Don't worry! Our analysts are monitoring your planet and the Earthlings very precisely. Your people are doing well," Thespon assured them.

Mac, who was silently listening and watching the entire conversation, didn't know what to say.

Mac deferentially told Thespon, "I sincerely beg your pardon for not obeying you as you sent Spectrovor to our planet to save us. Please save our fellow friends stuck in the ocean bed. They are still living like fish and mermaids."

Thespon told Earthlings to relax.

Trae Planet is Under Threat

"What's the purpose of our visit here in Trae? I mean, are we here accidentally or do you have any plans for us?" Jexter, in serious tone, asked Thespon.

Thespon answered, "Everything in the universe happens for a reason, my friend. Indeed, you will get to know your purpose of visit here pretty soon, Jexter. As of now, our planet Trae has been compromised by a demon planet named Diablocrox, known as devourer of planets," Thespon continued, saying, "It has already devoured several planets before marching in our Spectronom Galaxy. Ominoulada is a small part of Diablocrox which moved to the solar system to destroy Earth. If we are unable to stop Diablocrox from entering our planet then it will be the end of days. Our prime task is to stop Diablocrox."

"How you gonna achieve that? I hope you might have super-advanced weapons, missiles better than those of Earth, capable of destroying Diablocrox," Jexter curiously asked.

Thespon, in a trembling voice, grumbled, "Diablocrox cannot be destroyed. Our missiles, supersonic weapons won't have any effect on it. Diablocrox is made of Xenollium metal which is unbreakable. Even nuclear super-advanced missiles cannot break it."

Jexter promptly said, "What kind of metal is that? That metal does not even exist in the periodic table."

"You are right, Jex, that element does not exist in the periodic table of our planet either." Thespon further added, "Diablocrox can only be stopped if we can deceive Diablocrox."

Thespon continued, "As Diablocrox is moving in linear path through the intergalactic mirror, our planet Trae needs to make a parabolic move in our orbit to ward off the Diablocrox."

Jexter, Shelly and Mac listened with great zeal but the last point made by Thespon seemed unrealistic.

Shelly interrupted, "How is your planet going to make the parabolic move? We all know you possess supernatural powers. Does that also imply you have control over your planetary movements?"

Thespon clarified. "No, we don't have control over our planetary movements. But there is only one solution. Fortunately, the star Infinitum from our galaxy is coming near to our planetary orbit this weekend and this transit will last for 90 days. During this time Trae will be under the direct force field of Infinitum which will make Trae move in parabolic manner around its orbit and thus will be able to deceive the Diablocrox."

Jexter, Shelly and Mac now understood what Thespon just explained.

The Spectropeans and the Earthlings were anxiously awaiting the impending attack of Diablocrox. Within a week, the Spectropeans confirmed they saw the demon planet Diablocrox from their space research centre marching towards Trae's orbit. Fortunately the star Infinitum came closer to Trae's orbit and with the help of force field generated by Infinitum over Trae, Trae made a dynamic parabolic move and successfully managed to fox Diablocrox as predicted by Thespon. The supreme Infinitum thus saved planet Trae from being devoured by Diablocrox.

All the Spectropeans were riding in joy. Thespon threw a lavish party in his villa and asked the Earthlings Jexter, Shelly and Mac to be his guests of honor.

The Earthlings were obliged to be part of the celebration. The Earthlings met Jezebel, Thespon's wife who arranged a gala dinner. Jezebel, in a gorgeous queenly attire greeted Jexter, Shelly and Mac. Shelly also got stupefied seeing her lookalike and so were Jexter and Mac. Jezebel and Shelly had a long friendly chat in person. Jexter and Mac in the meantime showed their concerns to Thespon for their people stuck under ocean, living as fishmen and mermaids.

Thespon promised them he had already sent volunteers from Spectrovor near to the sunken ship where the Earthlings were residing in the underwater world of Earth. They were closely monitoring them and protecting them from sea predators. The city was in a jubilant mood as it was saved by imminent attack of Diablocrox. It was a festive time for the Spectropeans. All the Spectropeans were chanting the following slogans with drums, trumpets buzzing around.

"One two three four!"

"Infinitum always protects us for sure!"

"Diablocrox now out of sight!"

"Let's party all night!"

While all the Spectropeans were celebrating all night, some strange sightings were made at the other end of the city. The keeper of the city through his radar saw some strange creature crawling in the dark. Before he could do anything, he was ambushed by the creature and he fell dead on the ground. The city was once again under imminent attack by invaders which the Spectropeans were unaware of. Thespon got notification in his gadget immediately. As soon as he didn't get any response from keeper when he called the keeper, Thespon surmised something fishy had happened. He quickly sent signals from research lab to his people to be alert. Mac, Jexter and Shelly could sense some danger ahead.

Jexter asked Thespon about the alertness. Thespon told the Earthlings to stay calm. The strange creatures flying and jumping around came fast to the party zone and surrounded the place and told the Spectropeans to surrender.

The Spectropeans saw those creatures in horror. Those creatures looked like black demons' heads of skull and limbs like those of a reptile. They were breathing out fire from their noses. One of them came in front and asked, "Who's your leader, Spectropeans?"

"Here I am! Thespon! Leader of Spectropeans," said Thespon and took his weapon as if war would happen any time.

The demon creature roared, "I serve Diablocrox. Along with me are my comrades. We are known as Croxions. Diablocrox needs to feed on all matter that comes its way for survival. Only your planet Trae managed to deceive Diablocrox. You will pay for this, Spectropeans."

Saying this, the demon creature flew away along with its companions and echoed, "We will be back soon. Get ready for the battle."

Soon they disappeared in the dark sky.

Thespon knew this would not be an easy battle. He was wondering how these demon creatures landed on Trae planet in spite of deceiving the Diablocrox.

Thespon Calls for Infinitum

He knew their weapons were not sufficient to defeat those Croxions as they were all made of Xellonium metal. They again needed the help of Infinitum for a solution.

He gave orders to his soldiers to be ready for war and they could not win this war unless they got the divine intervention of their star Infinitum which was controlling the Spectronom Galaxy. Mac, Jexter and Shelly followed Thespon back to his place. Thespon went inside his artillery zone. Mac, Jexter and Shelly followed Thespon. He opened a safe containing only supersonic guns. A very bright and dazzling sword named Victor was embedded in the crystal chamber of the same safe. He pulled the sword with great difficulty.

The moment he took the sword, the entire place was dazzling like diamonds. He carried the sword Victor outside the place and came in the middle of a field and chanted,

"Thy Grace!
The Spectropeans once more
under severe threat.

Thy help is needed!
We need to defeat Diablocrox,
whatever it might take."

While chanting the spell, he lifted his sword to the east of Trae planet, which was the direction for Infinitum. His sword clashed in thunder from sky and an ethereal human from the east came in front of them. He was of god-like stature, wearing a big cloak, emitting light all through his body and having a golden stick on his hand and a golden crown on his head. Thespon introduced others to this ethereal human standing in front and said, "This is Infinitum! God of our Galaxy Spectronom," and turned to Infinitum and bowed down.

"Oh Lord! I beg your pardon to call you in such untimely hour. Diablocrox threat isn't over yet. They threatened to destroy our planet. We can't win this war as we don't have the solution to destroy the Xellonium metal. We need your assistance here."

Infinitum became thoughtful for a moment and in a sagacious tone said, "Call Zen and tell him to move around the planet Optix in our Spectronom Galaxy. He will find a pool of debris. He should collect those particles as much as he can. He must bring this debris and pour it into the Tifkiz Creek River, then use the compound generated in contact with Tifkiz and load the compound in your supersonic gun. This compound, when fired along with the bullets of supersonic gun, will be able to destroy the Diablocrox and any particles associated with it."

Thespon seemed happy after listening to what Infinitum said. He said, "Thank you, my lord! We will follow your orders without any delay."

Infinitum immediately left. Thespon summoned Zen, who was the most super-advanced Robot of the planet Trae, embedded with Artificial Intelligence. Zen was asked to perform his task and Zen immediately flew up into the sky and started moving towards the planet Optix and saw the pile of debris on its path. He collected the debris as much as he could and came back to Trae planet. He went to the Tifkiz Creek and put the debris in a big box and immersed it under the water bed. He kept it there for a whole night.

The next morning he lifted the box of debris from the water and opened the box and the debris were turned into thick viscous fluid with blue flames, generating a very high temperature. Thespon told everybody this was the compound which they would use and load in the weapon to destroy the Diablocrox demons, as this could dissolve the Xellonium metal which the Croxions were made of. Thespon told the Earthlings to stay away from the fight as their lives were precious for Thespon. Jexter retaliated by saying they would definitely participate in the battle on behalf of Spectropeans as Earthlings were indebted to Trae in some manner. Thespon was reluctant but Shelly, Mac and Jexter finally convinced Thespon that they would be proud to take part in the war. Everyone geared up to get ready for the battle against the Diablocrox demons, the Croxions.

Spectropeans Fight Croxions

Two days passed. There was no commotion of any sort in the planet Trae. In the third night, they could see those demon Croxions coming in masses from the sky.

They were planning to burn the planet. They were pouring fire from their noses. Here comes the order from Thespon. "Attack Diablo!"

Every Spectropeans including Mac, Jexter and Shelly started shooting those creatures using the supersonic guns. It was a brutal war. Both sides were going side by side.

One of the demon creatures jumped on Shelly and held her neck tightly from behind, but Shelly managed to topple the creature by her strong hands and kill it by triggering the bullet in time.

Jexter fought a fierce battle and saved the lives of Spectropeans. Mac got injured by a Croxion but Jexter in the nick of time saved him and went to fight with several Croxions. Jexter used all kind of weapons: dagger, sword, pistol, supersonic weapons. He even fought with bare hands with the demons and, in fact, faced the brunt of fire poured from the mouth of the demon. Thespon was very impressed with the spirit shown by the Earthlings. Finally, Spectropeans were able to defeat the demons from Diablocrox, claiming their supremacy in the Spectronom Galaxy.

After their win they were hailing Infinitum for being again their savior. Thespon also lauded the fight shown by the Earthlings, especially Jexter. Jexter was so happy to see Shelly putting up such a brave fight. Jexter planted a kiss on Shelly's forehead, appreciating her courage on the battlefield. Mac's injury was treated by Spectropean with utmost care and he was recovering pretty fast.

Who is Sprinkle Sparkle?

Now Jexter asked Thespon when would they go back to normal life. Thespon responded by saying their planet Trae was currently out of danger but they would make sure the Earthlings would be safe and find a permanent place for survival on Earth. They soon went to the spacelab to monitor what was happening on Earth.

The Earthlings were still living inside the sunken ship as water species. Jexter and Mac looked worried. Thespon looked into the magical glass mirror and said, "Look there! The place deep down the southern hemisphere near to Antarctica looks promising for humans to dwell. As the places all submerged under ocean, if by any miraculous movements of Earth's gravitational force, the tectonic plates near Antarctica with submerged city or town under water gets lifted above the water, then we could have a solution for the Earthlings' survival. Earth currently is in nascent state after the asteroid attack. It might undergo further changes and if some miracles happen, it can be a boon to the humans and can lead to source of dwelling on Earth. Till then, let's bring the Earthlings to our planet. We can monitor the status of Earth day by day."

Thespon ordered his soldiers who were navigating underneath the ocean near the sunken ship to bring back the Earthlings through the gateway of vacuum, the wormhole to the Spectronom Galaxy through which Jexter, Mac and Shelly came to Trae planet. The Spectropean soldiers navigating in the Earth's ocean bed near the sunken ship took the Earthlings to the wormhole and the hundred Earthlings came to the Trae planet of the Spectronom Galaxy.

Jexter, Shelly and Mac sat together in Thespon's private guest room and discussed how long they were going to stay on this alien planet. They needed to go back to the planet Earth and start a new civilization. For that, nature had to give them support. Until now they could only see the ruins of planet Earth, not a single island or landmass left congenial for survival of human species. Thespon assured them that their analysts were optimistic about the new land which may get uplifted very soon by Earth's gravitational force, which he showed them in their space lab. Thespon looked at the Earthlings and said "Don't worry, Earthlings. Come with me. You need to meet someone before you go back to Earth." Jexter and Shelly followed Thespon.

Thespon took them for a drive in the city outskirts. Suddenly he stopped near a highway where there was no sign of any vehicles, no traffic. He went near the traffic signal and knelt down and said, "Please show us your presence, our guiding lord." Within seconds a white horse appeared from nowhere. It looked divine in every angle. It bore a similar, uncanny, charisma to that of the Infinitum.

"This is Sprinkle Sparkle," uttered Thespon with utmost reverence. "He is no ordinary horse. Sprinkle Sparkle will take you guys for a ride. You will never regret the trip." Jexter and Shelly looked confused but decided to take a ride on Sprinkle Sparkle.

"This horse seems so pure, serene. I have never seen such a horse in my life. We will definitely take a ride on this horse," said Jexter in excitement. Shelly nodded her head. Thespon looked happy and left the place.

Sprinkle Sparkle Takes Jexter and Shelly for a Tour

Jexter and Shelly started moving around Sprinkle Sparkle and were amazed by the beauty of the horse. They were moving around for some time when suddenly they heard, "Jex, Shelly, get upon me without further delay. Let me show you my planet."

"Who's it? Shelly! Is it you?" said Jexter, looking at Shelly.

"Nope! It's not me," said Shelly.

Jexter and Shelly looked at each other, baffled. The horse turned around and looked straight at them and said, "It's me, dear Earthlings."

Jexter and Shelly jumped onto their feet, shocked, and at the same time said, "The horse talks."

Before they were about to ask any further questions of Sprinkle Sparkle, the horse ordered them, "Get into my back quickly. I will show you my planet." Jexter and Shelly jumped on the horse's back and horse started running fast. Sprinkle Sparkle, running at lightning speed, asked Jexter and Shelly to hold tight. Jex and

Shelly were having this surreal feeling. The horse rode to the end of the city near a cliff: down below lay a sea. While the horse came near the cliff, Jex and Shelly were tensed as they could see the end of the cliff. Before they could ask Sprinkle Sparkle to stop, they saw themselves high in the air on the horse's back after crossing the cliff, and a pair of wings appeared from the horse's back and they were flying over the sea. Jexter and Shelly now realised this was a divine horse.

The horse kept flying for quite some time. It crossed the oceans, the mountains, the trees, the clouds. Jexter and Shelly felt that they were dreaming. What a thrill they were having! The horse made a landing on a dense forest. The forest also looked unreal. It consisted of trees with beautiful flowers, butterflies and delicious fruits. The ground was filled with the leaves which made the place look more ethereal. Jexter and Shelly got down from the horse. Jexter immediately climbed up the tree and plucked some fruits and some flowers. He hid the flowers in his pocket. He climbed down and offered Shelly some fruits. Shelly started eating hungrily and Jexter too ate with great zest. Sprinkle Sparkle in a low voice murmured, "Where are the flowers? Won't you give them to Shelly?"

Shelly was surprised and asked Jexter if that was true. Jexter smiled and took the flowers from his pocket and gifted to Shelly. Shelly was elated and so was Jexter. "You are omniscient, Sparkle. How would you know I hid those flowers for Shelly?" asked Jexter.

Sprinkle Sparkle neighed and blurted, "Come on, Jexter, Shelly, sit down here. We need to talk." Jexter and Shelly while eating their fruits came and sat down.

Shelly gushed, "You beautiful divine horse. Tell us something about yourself before we say something about us."

"As you know my name is Sprinkle Sparkle. I am the torch bearer for all the big events in Spectronom. I am also the guiding light of the people on this planet Trae. If someone loses their way out, I guide them to safety. I know the entire planet. I am one of the important keepers of this planet. I also have some extraordinary powers which I use for the betterment of people on my planet."

Jexter now replied, "That's enough for us. The moment we saw you, we felt you are no ordinary horse. But do you know who we are?"

Sprinkle Sparkle promptly answered, "You are Earthlings. You have been here for temporary shelter in our planet. But you need to go to Earth as soon as possible as Earth needs you more than us. You must be wondering why I am saying this. You will get to know the reason at the very right moment."

Jexter put his hand over his head and kept on scratching his hair and babbled, "I know Earth needs me. I am no supernatural like you. But I will definitely go back to Earth and make it a living place as it used to be. I am going to build a new civilization." Shelly felt proud of Jexter but said nothing.

Sprinkle Sparkle jumped up high in the sky, signifying he too believed Jexter could salvage the human civilization on planet Earth and declared, "Jexter, Shelly! My blessings will always be bestowed upon you." Jexter and Shelly bowed down to Sprinkle Sparkle to show their respect. In return Sprinkle Sparkle asked Jexter if he could see a key hanging on his neck. Jexter looked into the horse's neck and found one bright shining key attached. Sprinkle Sparkle ordered Jexter to take the key as a gift which was related to unlocking the future of Earth. Jexter took the key and looked closely. Jexter was surprised and asked how to unlock the future of Earth using this key.

"As of now, I can only say this. You need to find out how you are going to use this key on Earth. That's what I can say at the moment," Sprinkle Sparkle explained. Jexter was perplexed by the answer given by Sprinkle Sparkle. He went into deep thought and kept thinking about how he could use the key.

The horse asked them to get into its back and they would be moving back to Thespon's place. Sprinkle Sparkle flew back fast and reached Thespon's office.

Earthlings Bid Adieu to Thespon

When they got down from the horse's back and tried to look back, the horse disappeared in the sky. They could see Thespon coming towards them in excitement and he asked them to come to his lab. They went to his spacelab where a specialist was deeply examining the planet Earth from various angles. Then he pointed to one of the regions in the southern hemisphere near the South Pole and said, "Look there! It seems an unknown landmass is visible. The Earth went through a fast transformation and the landmass submerged below got lifted pretty soon. Only thing is that we have to find whether the land is fit for survival." Thespon asked the specialist to zoom in on the place. The specialist zoomed in and they saw indeed a landmass covered with snow amidst the ocean. It was full of pine trees. Jexter thought the presence of trees is good sign of land. They need to make the land congenial for living and also try plantation of crops to make the land suitable for irrigation. Jexter whispered, "Thespon, you must send all of us right now to that place on Earth. We will try to make that land best for living on Earth."

"Sounds good. But do you want Spectropeans to come along with you and help you build the land?" Thespon asked Jexter. Jexter told he would like to build a kingdom on Earth all by his effort. But he would always be grateful to Spectropeans, people of Trae planet for the help they provided so far. Thespon responded he was proud of Jexter and warned him to be aware of unknown challenges that the Earthlings might face back on Earth while they start building a kingdom in the only landmass visible so far.

He further added that Jexter should not hesitate to use the supersonic gun and use it to communicate with Trae if any help was required. Any jeopardy in Jexter's life can be detrimental to Thespon's in Trae planet, so Jexter needed to be very careful.

Jexter was thinking of challenge of building the kingdom on Earth but in reality the challenge is completely different. Thespon suddenly asked Jexter, "Keep the key which Sprinkle Sparkle gave you as it will be pivotal for you to unleash a better future in Earth."

Jexter was surprised and tried to find the key in his pocket but to his dismay, he couldn't. Shelly put her hands on Jexter and said, "Here's the key, Jex. The moment you climbed back onto Sprinkle Sparkle it nearly fell, but I managed to hold and grab the key."

Jexter was happy and inquisitively asked Thespon, "What's so special about the key? The key is from Trae planet. How could we use it on planet Earth?"

Thespon simply told him to keep the key and said, "Who knows? The key may come handy to you and your Earthlings. Nobody knows."

Jexter again got puzzled as he got the same response from Thespon regarding the key. Whatever be the case, Jexter felt he would definitely find the answer to the key all alone.

Jexter, Shelly and Mac, along with a hundred Earthlings, started the journey to Earth.

Jexter, Mac and Shelly Return to Earth

They moved to the same deserted island from where they came to Trae planet by a wormhole connected from the bottom of Earth's ocean bed. They just reached Earth's ocean bed and reached exactly at the same place in the bottom of the sea with dense fog. They immediately turned into fishmen and mermaids, the power which they still possess kept intact, swam across the sunken ship where all the Earthlings gathered and by the help of a digital mirror attached with the supersonic gun, Jexter studied the longitude and latitude of the designated place of landmass. He, along with the other Earthlings, headed towards that landmass. It was indeed a long strenuous journey for the Earthlings, they were swimming nearly half the diameter of the Earth, almost 4000 miles to get to the landmass. They swam for weeks to reach there. They finally got into the designated island. Everyone transformed into humans and everyone thanked Jexter for being the true guide for them. Jexter asked everybody to have their full cooperation to build this a perfect place of habitat. He kept looking at the pine trees.

"Did you see those trees? Isn't it weird?" Jexter asked Shelly.

"Yes, I see those trees. Nothing looks weird to me."

"Look closely."

"Oh my gosh! The leaves are pitch black, how come the leaves are not green?"

"That's what I am saying," said Jexter.

Mac and all Earthlings were also wondering how come all the leaves of the trees were black. Jexter looked worried but he asked everyone to stay away from the trees. They got to explore the place. They flocked together in a group and moved ahead to explore the landmass. The entire place was full of pine trees. No other trees or any land suitable for irrigation was found. They crossed the snowy landmass and came to a normal landmass but miles away: no roads were found. While walking, Jexter suddenly found a cave within landmass, penetrating deep down into the soil.

Earthlings Explore an Uninhabited Island on Earth

Everyone was shocked to see a strange spiral-shaped cave.

Mac yelled "Don't go near to the cave, we never know what can be inside."

"No worries! I will go inside and have a look inside the cave. If anything is unusual, I will let you know," Jexter confidently said.

Shelly, with a worried look on her face, warned Jexter to be careful. Jexter went inside the dark cave with his supersonic gun and he could see everything by the torch embedded within the gun. He kept moving and suddenly he felt that his legs were not touching the ground and when he tried to put his other foot in the ground, he felt as if he was falling down. He kept falling down and fell into a lake. He swam up and saw a big cave, lit by will-o'-the-wisp. He was surprised, but not shocked. He swam to the rocks and stood up and felt something precious could be found inside the cave. He started walking inside when suddenly he heard the feeble voices of Shelly and Mac shouting together, "Jexter. Where are you? Everything okay?"

Jexter yelled, "Everything fine over here, no need to worry. I may take some time to come out. You guys don't come inside."

Shelly got angry and yelled, "We are also coming there. It's been long time you went inside." Shelly came forward and asked Mac to join her.

Mac responded to Shelly, "Let me look after my mates outside the cave. Good luck and notify us if there is any problem inside."

Shelly rushed inside the cave and just like Jexter, she fell below and plunged into the lake. She swam up only to see Jexter holding her tight and brought her back to the shore. Shelly was very angry with Jexter for not letting her know there was no staircase or path to the bottom of the cave. Jexter was now so deep down on the land inside an undiscovered cave. They started moving ahead together and exploring the place. They could only see lake and ice and the same pine trees which they had seen outside the cave. Suddenly Shelly saw a creature run in front of her. She couldn't see exactly what the creature was. She just saw the tail of the creature. The tail was quite long. Shelly immediately notified Jexter. Jexter also felt somebody already here before them. When he walked closer, he could hear some noises. The noise became more audible. Shelly was scared but brave enough to walk side by side with Jexter.

"Anybody trying to trick with us has to face consequences," Jexter shouted back, holding his supersonic gun. He got no response. He walked ahead inside and saw a huge door locked from outside. "Where the creature gone if the door is locked from outside?" Jexter thought.

Shelly started staring above the walls and the giant door. Astonishingly, the door and the walls had signs of stars and different symbols encrypted all over it. Shelly notified Jexter about it. Jexter told Shelly that might be the secret symbol of something. They needed to decode that. They tried hard to unlock the door, but couldn't. It seemed the door had not been opened for years. Jexter looked at Shelly and smiled. Shelly was amused and asked the reason behind his smile. Jexter told that he has the supersonic gun and still they were foolishly putting effort into unlocking the door. "What does that mean?" Shelly asked.

"Of course, I am going to break this door with this gun. Why put in so much effort?" Jexter answered.

Shelly grinned. Jexter fired at the door and the door broke apart. They went inside and it was like a palace but looked like a haunted one. The entire place was covered with spider webs. They were still wondering where the creature disappeared. They tried to look back. The moment they looked back, they saw the parts of the broken door astonishingly merged into one and locked them in the palace room from behind.

The Devil Maze

Jexter and Shelly now confirmed that was a haunted place. Something was inside it and it was looking for them. Shelly and Jexter stood alert, locked inside the palace hall. Jexter shouted to the walls, "Show yourself! I am not scared." Shelly held Jexter tightly. No response, as if everything was normal. They moved ahead, exploring the hall. As they moved inside they could hear voices and voice intensity was getting louder and louder. Jexter, holding his gun, started moving fast, leaving Shelly behind. After moving forward a bit, he just looked aside and saw Shelly was missing. He jumped and looked back and saw Shelly was tossed up in the air by a whirlwind generated in the floor of the hall and Shelly asked for help. Jexter ran to get hold of Shelly but Shelly flew across and hit the wall and miraculously vanished in one of the walls. Jexter was stunned and his blood froze but he was not scared. He would find Shelly at any cost. He tried to hit the walls and called for Shelly, but no response. Again in the walls he saw the same secret codes which he saw inside the cave before entering there. He felt that the code would reveal secret related to this haunted place. It could be the pathfinder in locating Shelly. Mac along with the other Earthlings were anxiously waiting for Jexter and Shelly outside. They had no idea what happened inside the cave. Jexter now trying to use his brain power. He, being a scientist, tried to break the wall inside which Shelly disappeared. His gun was not able to break it as he tried a few shots. Now he tried to pen down all the symbols in the floor which were available in the wall and tried to find correlation between them. He couldn't find any clues even after studying the symbols for long time. Suddenly he was using his cryptography skills to decode the letters of the symbols. He clearly knew this code could be decoded if he had all the symbols in place. He was trying to put together all symbols and he could see some symbols which he had drawn on the floor interchanged their positions miraculously. He knew he was near to cracking the code but he felt one symbol was missing to generate a three-dimensional octagonal door. He tried to search for any missing symbols which he might have missed incorporating but he couldn't find any new symbol on the door walls. He closed his eyes and started to think with deep concentration. He could hear a very soft feeble voice. "I am here, Jexter, They took me." Jexter tried to concentrate but failed again and he realised that was Shelly's voice as they had power of telepathy which was given to them by the Spectropeans. But why couldn't he hear her voice clearly? Jexter was now assured that he had to break the code to find Shelly. He again started searching for symbols relentlessly till he noticed his supersonic gun. He could see a small symbol on the back of the gun that looked just like the symbols on the walls. He then tried to write down that symbol on the floor for the missing connection for the octagonal door. The moment he was done with filling up the last symbol, an illusionary octagonal door appeared from nowhere. He stepped inside the door and soon found himself in an unknown place. The place was like a crystal maze. He could only see he was surrounded by multiple mirrors. He closed his eyes again to focus. Now he again heard the same soft voice of Shelly, this time more prominent and clear. "Jexter! I am trapped. Come and save me! They are going to kill me."

Jexter responded through his mind "Hold on, Shelly. I will get you out wherever you are trapped. Just tell me, where exactly are you situated?"

"In one the mirrors of the crystal maze," gasped Shelly.

"I have already arrived in this unknown place. I will find you for sure," murmured Jexter.

Jexter Meets a New Enemy

Jexter started hitting every mirror and yelled loudly, "Shelly! Are you there?" No response came. Among the hundreds of mirrors, Jexter noticed one mysterious mirror which was completely different. He went nearby and kept staring until suddenly a strange old fragile lady came out from the mirror. "Who is she? Is some poor lady trapped in this unknown place?" murmured Jexter on his own.

The lady looked at Jexter and said, "Oh! Jexter, you came."

"How you know my name?" Jexter asked, shockingly.

"I am Shelly! You forgot me." The old lady started crying. Jexter was confused and couldn't understand what was going on.

Before Jexter could question the old lady further, the old lady said a sorceress changed her into an old lady.

"How come you got released from the mirror? Where is the sorceress?" Jexter asked suspiciously.

"The moment you arrived here with your pure soul in this place, the evil sorceress left," replied the old lady.

Jexter still couldn't believe what she was saying. He put his hands on his face and tried to focus. While thinking hard, again he heard the voice of Shelly asking for help. Jexter knew now the old lady was not Shelly. The old lady was pretending to be Shelly. Now Jexter looked at the old lady and ranted, "Tell me your real identity, old lady. You are not Shelly. Before I pull my trigger, reveal." The old lady gave a delirious laugh at Jexter which gave shivers in the spine of Jexter. The old lady immediately transformed into a sorceress with a deep black scar near her cheekbone. Jexter took a shot at the sorceress. The bullet hit the lady but no blood came out. Jexter was baffled. The lady then cast a magic spell and Jexter was tied up by the spider webs in the ground and he nearly got wrapped up by the web. The old lady yelled, "Both of you rot here till you die," and disappeared from the place.

Jexter Rescues Shelly

Jexter was relieved a bit as he now got confirmed that Shelly was also here. He tried to free his arms from the spider web but couldn't. He moved his body and hit a pot, which got broken. A squirrel came out from the pot and started eating the web where Jexter was trapped. The squirrel silently bit the web for quite some time. Jexter stood silent and he could hardly see anything as his face was also wrapped in spider webs, but he understood some small creature trying to eat the wrapper. Now Jexter could free his hands, the moment he freed his hands he tore apart the web wrapper from his face and saw the squirrel, which was biting the wrapper and helped him free from the spider web. Jexter smiled at the squirrel and got hold of the squirrel and the squirrel quickly climbed on Jexter's shoulder and sat down there peacefully. Jexter smiled and said, "I got a new friend in this unknown place." Jexter tried to shoot the walls in order to find Shelly but the weapon had no impact. He again thought, if his supersonic gun didn't have any impact on the mirror, how could this be broken? He looked at the squirrel and he saw the squirrel started running quickly towards the mirror from which the sorceress appeared before. Jexter followed the squirrel and went inside the mirror.

It was dark inside. Jexter switched on his gun light and could see a big red button inside. He switched on the button immediately and saw all the mirrors opened and demons coming out from the mirror. Jexter took his supersonic gun and started shooting them. Jexter managed to defeat those demons but they did not die. They were lying in the ground, some wounded. Jexter saw the demons were same ones from Diablocrox against whom he fought for Trae planet in Spectronom Galaxy. "How the Croxions arrived on Earth? Was he on Earth? Or on demon planet Diablocrox?"

He started searching all the mirrors. All the mirrors were empty as all the demons came out. He looked at the squirrel once again and the squirrel pointed one of his fingers to one of the mirrors. Jexter said, "You want me to go and check that mirror?" The squirrel nodded his head. Jexter quickly went inside the mirror and indeed found Shelly lying unconscious. Jexter got scared and quickly trying to revive Shelly by rubbing her hands, her feet. Shelly came back to her senses and held Jexter tightly.

"Why've you taken so much time to come here?"

"I wouldn't have found you if this friend of mine didn't help," Jexter pointing his hand towards the squirrel and the squirrel came to Jexter's shoulder once again.

"This is my new friend who helped me find you," Jexter said.

Shelly looked at the squirrel and said, "We owe this squirrel a lot. It must stay with us." Shelly then planted a kiss on the cheek of the squirrel.

"How you arrived in this unknown place? What is the name of this place? Are we still on Earth?" Jexter fired up the questions to Shelly in one breath.

"That old witch took me into this place from the walls last time when we were together. She was saying this is probably the Earth's crust and she is going to have vengeance on Earthlings. I don't know why she said that. I tried to ask her where she belonged and why she wanted to harm the Earthlings. She didn't respond and imprisoned me behind those mirrors," Shelly yelped.

"I now get the point, Shelly. The witch must be from Diablocrox. You can see the demons lying here wounded," Jexter anxiously said.

"Oh no! Not again! The battle still not over. What do they want on Earth? How they came to Earth?" Shelly groaned.

"Now I know why Thespon wished us luck with all the upcoming challenges," Jexter grumbled.

"How are we going back to the place we were before? We have to get back soon to our people and protect them from the sorceress as they are in severe danger. How are we going back to the place from where we came? How did you arrive in this place?" Shelly screeched.

"Don't worry. I came here by my genius brain. Remember I am scientist," bragged Jexter.

"If you know the way out from here, then don't waste any time," Shelly cried.

"Give me some time, Shelly. I need to draw some stuff," Jexter said.

"What stuff you are going to draw and what for?" an inquisitive Shelly asked.

"Hold on. You will get to see now," Jexter replied.

Jexter started drawing the cryptographic symbols which he had drawn before to arrive in this unknown place. Jexter has got that supernatural memory power and he remembered every symbol. Initially he was struggling to draw. Then he closed his eyes and started drawing those symbols on the floor.

Shelly now could recognize some of the symbols and asked Jexter curiously, "These are the symbols we saw in the walls before coming here. How do you remember those symbols? What are these symbols for?"

"Stay silent! Let me focus," Jexter interrupted Shelly.

Jexter scratching his head and had drawn all the symbols. But nothing happened as before. Jexter expected the octagonal door to appear as he finished writing the symbols in a logical manner. No door appeared. There seemed to be some problem with the symbols. Did Jexter miss out any symbol? Jexter was a confident scientist, he didn't forget stuff which he saw. He skimmed the symbols one at a time and could see they were perfectly correlated. Still nothing happened. Jexter's cryptographic skills couldn't be wrong.

Escape from Devil Maze

The squirrel was making noises and it lay on Shelly's lap. Shelly held it tightly, not letting it go. The squirrel suddenly jumped off the lap of Shelly and sat on the floor where Jexter was drawing. Jexter tried to push the squirrel away but the squirrel sat down. The squirrel was looking at the symbols drawn. Then it came to the last letter, which contained the symbol attached with the gun. It pointed its finger to that symbol. Jexter immediately understood the squirrel wanted to convey something.

"Is my last symbol wrong?" murmured Jexter. The squirrel kept scratching the last symbol.

Suddenly the squirrel jumped onto the first symbol. It kept scratching the first symbol. Again it jumped back to the last symbol. This kept going for some time. The squirrel jumped back and forth between first and last symbol. Jexter now understood his mistake. He had to work in reverse to create the octagonal door.

"Jex! The squirrel is trying to say something," Shelly opined.

"I understood what the squirrel is trying to say. The squirrel is an angel," Jexter answered Shelly.

Jexter then started writing the symbols in reverse. Now, after drawing the entire stuff, the octagonal door appeared and Jexter pulled Shelly. Jexter pulled up the squirrel on his shoulder and they stepped into the door.

Immediately they found themselves back to the old place in the cave.

Shelly was amazed at Jexter's analytical skills. Shelly praised Jexter. "You are one hell of a genius."

Jexter took the squirrel on his shoulder and said, "This squirrel is our life saver. We have to know the real identity of the squirrel." Jexter sighed in relief and kissed the squirrel's cheek.

Jexter then told Shelly to get on the top of the cave on the island and find the people. Shelly warned Jexter about the impending threat of the old sorceress. They must quickly find a way on top of the island from the cave. They came exactly to the place in the cave where they glided down on the bottom of the cave. They shouted together looking upwards "Mac! You there! Help us getting out from the cave."

There was no response. Jexter and Shelly continued yelling at the top of their lungs but no response from the people. Jexter looked at squirrel and said, "Little angel! You've got any idea how we get on to the top?" The squirrel immediately ran to the walls of the cave and crawled up to the top and disappeared. Jexter and Shelly knew the squirrel definitely went for help. They waited a long time. Jexter was anxious as he was worried about the safety of the squirrel. After a long time waiting, Jexter and Shelly fell asleep in the cave, expecting the squirrel to return. Jexter, while taking a nap, got woken up by the squirrel. Jexter and Shelly were excited to see the squirrel back. They followed the squirrel and the squirrel took them near to the water. Jexter glanced at the crystal clear water and spotted a broken ladder below the water. The ladder was still in good enough condition to use. Jexter smiled at the squirrel. "You did it again, Angel." The squirrel jumped off the shoulder of Jexter. Shelly and Jexter climbed off the ladder and came outside the cave. They came out and couldn't find any Earthlings. Where the Earthlings gone? Were they being abducted by the sorceress? Jexter's mind was fluttered with these kinds of thoughts. It already became dark. Only stars were visible in the sky.

Shelly and Jexter started to search for people. They could see the pine trees ranging over long areas. It seemed that the trees grew in number since they were here. Jexter and Shelly yelled for Mac. No response from the trees. They walked for quite some time in the barren land until they were exhausted and fell asleep.

In the meantime, while Jexter and Shelly were asleep the demons of the sorceress came to Shelly and Jexter and carried them to a place hidden in between the dense pine trees and made them captives. Jexter and Shelly were so exhausted that they didn't realize they were been carried by the demons. The squirrel was sleeping inside the satchel of Shelly to feel warm.

Earthling Became Prisoners

Jexter woke up only to realize he was made captive by someone. Jexter tried to free his hands which were tied by chains.

He could see he was confined in a cave. The light of sun rays were falling into the cave and Jexter understood the cave would be from any of the mountains. How did he arrive here? He tried to find his gun and he found it missing. He searched for Shelly but couldn't find her.

He could see himself chained inside a vast cave where nobody could be seen. He was wondering who would have made him captive and where were Shelly and the Earthlings. No matter how pulverizing a situation Jexter was in, he was never scared and he always tried to face it with aplomb. He then thought of squirrel and thought that it might be nearby, but no trace of the miraculous squirrel was found. Jexter held his nerves and kept waiting. He kept waiting for long, long time and finally he could see three demons coming towards him. He was shocked to see the demons were none other than the soldiers of the demon planet Diablocrox. The same creatures gushing fire from their noses and having tail of a reptile. The three Croxions came to Jexter and unchained him from the walls, although Jexter's hands were tied. They then lifted Jexter on their shoulder and started carrying him. Jexter was silently watching. He didn't say a word. He was looking at the demons and observing them minutely.

Jexter was inundated with thoughts on how these Croxions came to Earth. Anyway, Jexter was carried for some time till the demons came near the end of cave. The cave ended at a point from where a waterfall started. Jexter was lifted down by the demon and Jexter stood up with his hands tied.

"Welcome, Jexter! So you managed to escape from the maze," the sorceress said.

"Who are you?" Jexter ranted.

"I am Claribel Hunt, Goddess of once-a-planet Diablocrox," screeched the sorceress.

"What do you want from Earth?" Jexter furiously asked.

"It's because of you our planet no longer exists. We came to Earth by Ominouloda and wanted to capture Earth. But you Earthlings managed to destroy a major chunk of Ominoulada, resulting in demolishing the majority of our species. But some of our species are here to capture and feed on your planet Earth for survival. We are going to make this Earth our new Diablocrox."

"That's never going to happen, evil lady. This planet belongs to us. You must leave this planet or you have to face the consequences," Jexter shouted back.

"Muahahaha," Claribel laughed. "You petty Earthling. Do you know my powers? Your planet is demolished. You have hundreds of people left alive. You are threatening me. Good joke."

She clapped and Jexter could see all the Earthlings, including Mac and Shelly, were tied up with a rope and floating above on the pile of fire.

Jexter's heart pounded. He immediately asked Claribel, "What's the deal? What do you want from me?"

"You are indeed a smart guy, Jexter," mocked Claribel. "You have to make me look younger. I look very old," Claribel ordered Jexter and started licking Jexter's cheek.

Jexter pushed her aside and yelled, "Back out, lady."

"Stay away from Jexter, you devil, I will kill you if you touch Jexter," ranted Shelly, ready to release the rope she was tied with, but she couldn't as the rope was too tight for her to escape.

Claribel stared at Shelly and gave an evil laugh. She kept laughing and looked at Jexter.

"So I got to know your weakness, Mr Handsome," Claribel said.

She ordered her soldiers to bring Shelly in front of her. They immediately went to the top and brought back Shelly.

Claribel, the New Evil Queen of Earth

When Shelly was brought, Jexter moved forward to get hold of Shelly. As soon as Jexter moved forward, Claribel cast a spell and Jexter was caged inside a glass house. Jexter tried to break the glass but couldn't. He could only see what was going on outside.

Shelly was held as a prisoner by the demons. Claribel came close to Shelly and lifted her finger. Claribel's fingernails were growing larger and she pierced her fingernail into the veins of Shelly's hand. Jexter shouted helplessly but he saw Shelly transforming into an old lady. Shelly fainted, seeing the transformation. Claribel ordered her demon soldiers to carry back Shelly and lock her in a separate cave. Jexter tried his best to break apart the glass cage but couldn't.

"You will die for this. If you don't transform Shelly to her old self, I swear you will not see the sunlight tomorrow," thundered Jexter.

Claribel at evil tone said, "Calm down, scientist, you can't do anything. You are mere mortal.

"Now just listen to what I want you to do if you don't want to see your sweetheart die."

Jexter violently beat the glass cage in vain.

Claribel understood the situation of Jexter. She ordered him to go deep down the ocean bed and find the Praleosh, a luminous hypercube which they lost when the Ominoulada hit Earth.

Praleoshh is the source of power for Claribel and her demon comrades Croxions. Claribel didn't let Jexter know anything about Praleoshh. Claribel's intension was to use her evil powers and subjugate the people of Earth and make them her slaves.

"How soon do I need to be back here? Where's the location of the Praleoshh?" Jexter questioned.

"You need to be here by tomorrow's sunrise. You need to find it yourself. If you don't reach on time, your people will die one at a time. Oh yes! Your loved one will die last," laughed Claribel and freed Jexter.

Jexter, without wasting time, ran fast and suddenly stopped after running several yards and stared at Claribel with intense eyes. Claribel for the first time in her life got scared, looking at Jexter's expressive eyes.

Jexter Needs to Find Praleoshh

Jexter kept thinking of Shelly and vowed to kill the sorceress. How could he find the Praleoshh in such vast ocean in such short span? He just remembered the key which Sprinkle Sparkle gave him. When could he use this key? Was it to unlock some other box or is this related to Praleoshh? Several questions kept Jexter's mind flooded.

He went outside the cave and tried to find his supersonic gun. He couldn't find the gun as he was unable to trace the path from where he was picked up while he was unconscious.

Without the gun, he knew it was difficult to defeat the sorceress but he made a promise to himself that by tomorrow's dawn he would definitely slay the sorceress and her demon soldiers. He also tried to search for the squirrel which was out of sight for quite some time.

He knew the squirrel shouldn't be far away. Soon he saw some footmarks on the sand from the entrance of the cave to the path from which he came. He walked ahead for some time until he saw his squirrel nibbling on a fruit on the sand. Jexter got elated and the squirrel also jumped onto Jexter's shoulder. He walked ahead and tried to find the gun and fortunately he found his supersonic gun half submerged in the sand where the squirrel was sitting. He took the gun and came to the shore of the ocean and put down the squirrel on the ground and said, "Divine friend. Stay here. I will be back after some time. I cannot let you come with me."

Jexter then jumped into the water and soon transformed into a fishman and he started swimming across the ocean randomly. This journey in the ocean was going to be very challenging. Jexter knew it was impossible to find the Praleoshh by the next day's sunrise. Jexter fortunately managed to defeat the predators under the ocean, but he couldn't find any trace of any hidden object under the ocean bed. Suddenly he saw his gun was blinking some light and he could see a direction map was projected. Jexter now knew Thespon gave him the direction as the Spectropeans already detected the location of Praleosh. Jexter swam fast towards the direction and could finally see a luminous hypercube sitting at the ocean bed. With great strength he managed to lift Praleosh with the help of his gun, which acted as a lever, and swam really hard and finally managed to get back to the shore with the buoyant force of the sea. He transformed back to normal self and now it was taking a huge effort to move the Praleoshh on the land. He realized his jointed appendages while as fishman underwater, along with the help of the supersonic gun, helped him to lift this hypercube Praleoshh. He could not lift the Praleoshh on land. He could push this Praleoshh. He started inspecting the cube and saw the hypercube had a lock. He looked at the key given to him by Sprinkle Sparkle, which he was wearing as locket. Was this the key to unlock the mystery? Was this the key to unlock the future of Earth? He thought he would try with this key. He tried to unlock Praleoshh using the key. Nothing worked and Jexter became disappointed, thinking when would he going to use the mystery key he was given by Sprinkle Sparkle? He could see something was glowing inside the Praleosh. He tried to break the hybercube using his supersonic gun. The gun didn't have any effect on it. It remained intact. He would explore this hypercube later. He would definitely try to unlock the Praleoshh. But now he had an idea. He would not let this Praleoshh get into Claribel's hands and neither he would reveal the location of Praleoshh. He hid the Praleoshh near the shore. Now the time for vengeance had come. He decided to confront the evil sorceress. Only thing he was worried that the sorceress must have patience, otherwise the sorceress might harm the Earthlings if he didn't arrive in time.

Claribel Attacks Jexter

He entered the evil queen's chamber empty handed before sunrise. Claribel was surprised to see Jexter as she thought he might have died. Claribel promptly asked Jexter "Where's my Praleoshh? You know your time is over. It's about sunrise now and you still didn't have the Praleoshh."

"I brought it and kept it outside. First release all the Earthlings. Then I will give you Praleoshh," Jexter adamantly said.

"Very smart, you trying to fool me," Claribel giggled.

"If you don't release my people, you will never get back your Praleoshh," Jexter roared in confidence.

Claribel then politely questioned, "You don't trust me?"

"You? No way! You crazy devil," Jexter thundered.

"All right! I will release your people. Croxions, release the Earthlings," Claribel insisted.

Jexter kept waiting anxiously. After quite some time, he could see all the people were released and they left the cave. Jexter was happy, seeing his people freed. Mac came and hugged Jexter. Jexter also got emotional. He told the people to leave the place.

Jexter couldn't find Shelly in the crowd.

"Where's Shelly?" Jexter asked.

"She is on her way. We have given her proper medication to recover," Claribel said.

"Don't lie. Where is Shelly?"

In the meantime all the Earthlings left the cave and went together outside and waited for Jexter. Jexter was smelling something fishy.

"Bring back Shelly now," Jexter growled.

"Ha ha! First bring me the Praleoshh. I can't wait any more. Once you give me Praleoshh, Shelly will be here," Claribel said with an evil tone.

Jexter realized Claribel bluffed him and kept Shelly as prisoner. He would have his vengeance and time had come. Jexter politely asked Claribel, "Come with me this way. I will take you to the place where I have kept Praleoshh."

Claribel was excited and ordered Croxions to come along with them. In the meantime, Shelly got back to her senses but found herself tied up. She yelled from the top, "Jexter? where are you?"

Jexter responded, "Hold on Shelly! I will be back soon."

Claribel looked happy that Jexter was not so much caring for Shelly. They went ahead. They came to an unknown place outside the cave and Jexter told them to dig the ground.

He convinced them that he had kept Praleoshh underneath. Claribel believed Jexter and ordered the Croxions to dig the ground fast. The Croxions started digging the ground. Claribel curiously waited for the Praleoshh to be unearthed. Shelly in the meantime successfully untied herself and secretly followed Claribel. While Claribel was busy looking down at the ground which the Croxions were digging, Jexter leaped aside and, in a flash, took away the sword from a Croxion and drove it right into the heart of Claribel.

Claribel screeched and then collapsed. Jexter was happy as he had taken vengeance on the sorceress. He looked down the other side where the Croxions were digging deep down for the Praleoshh. Then he looked back at Claribel and saw Claribel was reviving fast and ever. There was no trace of blood anywhere. Jexter realized that the demon Claribel was immortal. How would he kill her? He lifted his supersonic gun hidden behind his shirt and started shooting Claribel. The supersonic gun had no effect on Claribel.

"You mortal human. Now face my wrath," thundered Claribel.

The entire environment shook as she yelled at Jexter. Strong rays of light from Claribel's eyes fell on Jexter's head and Jexter immediately fell on the ground where the Croxions were digging. "Bury him! There's no Praleoshh here. Jexter duped us. He must die and so will the Earthlings."

Shelly was quietly following them and when she saw Jexter was attacked by Claribel, she ran towards Claribel and held her by the neck, trying to choke her. But the Croxions from the ground came up and pulled back Shelly. The Croxions were about to kill Shelly when Shelly called for Jexter. Jexter lay numb on the ground. Claribel got relieved and ordered the Croxions not to kill Shelly. Claribel would make Shelly her slave along with the Earthlings. That would give her the most satisfaction as the reigning Queen on Earth.

Jexter Buried Alive

Claribel ordered the Croxions to bury Jexter within the ground they dug. Shelly was pulled by the Croxions and taken away as prisoner from the place. Shelly looked helpless and her heart nearly stopped beating as she could see Jexter being buried by the monsters. The Croxions buried Jexter and left the scene along with Claribel.

Jexter lay under the ground with his eyes closed. His heart was still beating. Suddenly Jexter came to his senses and he couldn't breathe. He realized he was buried and all the mud and sand were on his face and body. He tried to push the sand from his face and tried to lift himself up with stupendous effort. His body gave up but his mind didn't: if he didn't use his full power he would be buried alive. He kept moving his hands and legs to resurrect himself. The more he was removing the more sand and mud were pouring on his face.

In the meantime the squirrel came from nowhere, kept removing the sand under which Jexter was buried. It removed the entire sand and Jexter felt some external force had helped him to come out. He suddenly could feel the air outside and he lifted himself off the ground and he could see the squirrel removing the sand.

Jexter was elated and went to the squirrel and kissed the squirrel to show his gratification.

Outside the cave, the Earthlings were waiting for Jexter. But Jexter was not seen for a long time. Mac was anxious and told the Earthlings to calm down and have some patience.

Soon they could see Claribel come out of the cave, along with Croxions.

Claribel howled, "Earthlings. Your leader is dead. You all are my slaves. If you all want to survive, simply follow my orders."

All the Earthlings including Mac cried but didn't believe in Claribel's words.

Claribel Finds Praleoshh

The entire island became barren: no fruit, no flowers. All the trees were black. There was no vegetation. Jexter kept walking along with the squirrel to find Shelly. Claribel was now discussing with the Croxions about the location of Praleoshh. She thought Jexter never brought the Praleoshh from the ocean and she had to find that with the help of Croxions urgently. While discussing, Claribel saw a bright spark emanating from the sand near the shore. She quickly went there along with the Croxions and ordered the Croxions to dig the sand from where the light spark was generated. They started digging and Claribel jumped in happiness as she finally found the Praleoshh. The Croxions were also happy, beating their chests in happiness.

Claribel brought the hypercube and could see the lock. She told the Croxions to destroy the lock. The Croxions tried to break the lock but failed. Seeing this, Claribel herself tried to break the lock by casting magic spells and in the end she also failed. In the meantime severely injured Jexter came there with the squirrel on his shoulder walking with great difficulty. He laughed loudly and then shouted at Claribel, "You can never open the Praleoshh."

Jexter is Still Alive

Claribel was stunned to see Jexter alive, and murmured, "How is this possible? How is he alive?"

The Earthlings and Shelly were happy to see Jexter alive. Shelly could see Jexter nearly half dead, severely injured, taking small strides ahead with great difficulty.

Claribel ordered the Croxions to bring Jexter near to her.

The Croxions brought Jexter in front of Claribel. One single blow could end Jexter's life. Claribel in usual evil tone said, "I can see you managed to come alive. But you are already dead meat. You can do no harm to me. I am going to open this Praleoshh. Now I can understand indeed you bought the Praleoshh and tried to trick me. It says that you do have a solution to open this hypercube. That's the reason you didn't let me know where the Praleoshh was located. Now will you let me know the solution to unlocking this Praleoshh?"

Jexter stood silent. Claribel, running out of patience warned Jexter to let her know the solution to unlock the hypercube. Suddenly Claribel noticed the key on the neck of Jexter.

She snatched the key from Jexter's neck, thinking she had found the key to unlock the hypercube. She pushed Jexter back and used the key to unlock the Praleoshh. The key fitted inside but was unable to unlock the cube. She tried many times but realized the key was useless.

In a fit of rage, Claribel ordered the Croxions to kill Shelly. Shelly, held as prisoner, was about to be burnt alive by one of the Croxions. Jexter requested Claribel to spare Shelly as she had nothing to do it. If Claribel could take life of Jexter, Jexter would happily sacrifice his life for the Earthlings. Claribel in no mood to spare Shelly, thinking that Jexter was again hiding the solution of unlocking the Praleoshh. Jexter again tried to convince Claribel by saying, "I don't have any solution to unlock the Hypercube. You have to believe me. I am not hiding anything."

Jexter could sense the impending danger on the Earthlings decided to go near the hypercube and unlock it. He had no energy left but with his last and final effort, Jexter held the hypercube and put a mammoth effort into lifting the hypercube above. All the Earthling and the Croxions around were watching something extraordinary which they had never witnessed before. Jexter's flexible muscles were pumped up and he lifted the entire cube right above his shoulder and threw the hypercube to the ground, hard. Nobody was able to break hypercube ever before Jexter's attempt. The hypercube broke apart and the only thing left was a coral bracelet which glittered the place and a rainbow cast in the sky. Jexter immediately collapsed on the ground this time like a dead man. Was he dead?

Shelly cried in pain and so did the Earthlings. They could see Jexter sacrificed his life for them.

Praleoshh is Still a Mystery to Croxions

Claribel was so excited. Jexter had done something which the Croxions couldn't. Jexter broke the Praleoshh which contained the source of power. The rainbow of light sparked out of the box and the entire island was undergoing changes. After some time everyone realized the rays of light were actually turning the island into a barren island once again. The powers of the hypercube failed. Soon the trees which were blossomed and butterflies flying around turned into the same old black trees and bats started flying around. Seemed like it turned into dead city once again. Claribel had a violent outburst of anger and tried to cast her magic spells on the cube but to her dismay, they didn't have any effect on the surroundings.

The Earthlings realized this was end of civilization and now that Jexter was dead, there would be no savior. Shelly screeched, "See what you got, you evil sorceress? Even the cube is going against your spells and expectations. Now it's time for doom. We will die and so will you. You cannot save yourself."

Claribel didn't heed Shelly's words. She tried to cast her spells on the cube to work in her favour but nothing was going in her favour. The cube seemed cursed. She got mad in anger and ordered the Croxions to throw the dead body of Jexter on the water as Jexter's presence was distracting her. She didn't want to see Jexter's body on the island. While the Croxions threw Jexter up to the sky, towards the water near the shore, everyone saw Jexter's body fall like a dead leaf on the water near the shore. Claribel ran near the shore to confirm Jexter's body fell into the water. While returning near the Praleoshh, the hypercube they could see a small coral bracelet within the Praleoshh shining like a diamond.

Claribel Meets her Final Destiny

The Croxions moved near to the bracelet but as they came closer, they could not withstand the intensity of heat generated by the glow of the bracelet.

Claribel lambasted the Croxions. "You worthless morons. Can't even bring a small bracelet."

Claribel now herself decided to go and have the bracelet which she was yearning for, the last hundred years. She went near and with tremendous effort managed to get hold of the bracelet.

She had her evil laugh and demeaned the Croxions. She wore the bracelet. Within seconds, she screamed wildly as if she was going to die. The bracelet automatically pressed so tightly into the wrist of Claribel, she was groaning in pain. She tried to remove the bracelet but couldn't and the bracelet gripped Claribel tightly. Claribel ordered the Croxions to help her dismantle the bracelet from her wrist. The Croxions were scared as they knew they could not curb the power of the bracelet. They stepped backward. Claribel now understood her end was near and the bracelet was emitting its destructive powers and soon Claribel Hunt started decomposing and within minutes she turned into ashes and disappeared into the atmosphere.

The Earthlings were happy to see the end of the Evil Queen, Claribel. The moment Claribel died, Shelly transformed to her beautiful young self from old lady.

Resurrection of Jexter

"Wake up, Jexter," a voice murmured in Jexter's dream.

"Am I dead?" came Jexter's response in his dream sequence.

Jexter saw Sprinkle Sparkle hovering around him.

"I've lost the battle. Evil Claribel won. I couldn't make it. The key is with her. She unleased the evil force and conquered," Jexter said.

"No, Jexter, nothing is lost. The key is nothing. Even you tried. Did it work?

"Can't you see why Claribel tried to kill you? Why does she want your key?"

"The key which I gave you is just a decoy to the external world," Sprinkle Sparkle muttered in Jexter's dream. Then Jexter saw the squirrel in his dream, along with Sprinkle Sparkle in his dream.

"I am and I will always be there with you," muttered Sprinkle Sparkle.

Jexter understood that he was the chosen one and the squirrel was another avatar of Sprinkle Sparkle who was there with him throughout his journey on Earth. Sprinkle

Sparkle takes different forms during his incredible journey.

Jexter opened his eyes only to see Shelly in front of his eyes. Shelly was resuscitating Jexter.

Tears of happiness flowed from Shelly's eyes. Jexter could now understand Sprinkle Sparkle wanted to show him a path in his dream and he would have already been dead had Shelly not resuscitated him. Jexter stood up and moved towards the hypercube. The Croxions were stupefied to see Jexter alive.

Jexter went near to the bracelet and raised his right hand towards the bracelet and the bracelet flew and gripped Jexter's hand. Earthlings were tensed as Jexter might face the same fate as Claribel. Mac and Shelly folded their hands and prayed. The bracelet made a perfect fit to Jexter's hand. The moment it fitted tightly on Jexter's hand, lightning and thunder appeared and the rays of light from the bracelet spread over the sky. Jexter pointed the bracelet to the Croxions. The Croxions also faced the same fate as Claribel. They couldn't withstand the ray and decomposed to ashes. Earthlings were witnessing something incredible. They could see the entire barren island, filled with black pine trees, was now transformed into a super-advanced city. The skyscrapers, park, gardens lakes, bridges and office towers appeared: lands for irrigation and a huge castle appeared in front of them. The thunder stopped and the emanating rays from the bracelet also stopped.

Jexter, the King of Exalted Kingdom

Jexter smiled to himself and looked up to the sky and said, "Thank you dear Sprinkle Sparkle, Thespon. I know now why you didn't reveal the secret of unlocking the future of Earth. Along with my fellow Earthlings, we are indebted to you." Everyone looked up to the sky. They could see nothing but a pure sky above. But Jexter, Mac and Shelly saw Sprinkle Sparkle flying across the sky, who looked back at them. Jexter, Mac and Shelly together bid adieu to Sprinkle Sparkle with teary eyes. Sprinkle Sparkle flew above and disappeared and a huge block of clouds floated in the sky and read, "Good luck".

The Earthlings saw the caption in the clouds. Everyone bowed down to Jexter. Mac shouted and asked all the Earthlings, "Hail our king! the mighty Jexter Bladebrace."

Shelly's happiness knew no bounds. She reported back to Mac and said, "Mac, my friend. There's a little change in the name of our king. It's Jexter Bladebracelet now."

Mac smiled and so did Jexter. Jexter answered, "This victory is all of ours. I am no king, nor a ruler. I am your friend. Together we have to make this new civilization successful. Without your display of courage and cooperation, we wouldn't have achieved what we achieved today. We have a long way to go."

One of the Earthlings gently said, "But you are already our master, savior and king. It's nice for all of us to be friends of the king. You have to be king, as we are not educated enough to run a kingdom."

"All right! My friends, I will take up the responsibility, but Mac has to be my advisor," Jexter humbly asked the Earthlings. The Earthling nodded together. Jexter was so happy to see Shelly back to her younger self. Jexter now asked Shelly, "What are your thoughts?"

Shelly, without saying anything, held Jexter and kissed him. Jexter smiled and the Earthlings echoed together, "Shelly is our queen." Jexter, Shelly and Mac waved everybody and asked everyone to come with them to enter the castle.

Jexter could see his supersonic gun. He lifted the gun and could see a notification. "You made it. Congratulations. We are so proud."

The Earthlings asked, "What was that?"

Jexter responded, "The Spectropeans are proud of us and our dear friend Thespon congratulated us." They entered the castle together.

Thespon, while looking through his magical mirror, said to Jezebel, "Look! I said they would be successful."

He then smiled and switched off his magical mirror and said, "Earth has a capable king now and his name is Jexter Bladebracelet."